GOSIG

Adventures at the Fairground

Text: Karin Salmson
Illustration: Tony Wolf

GOSIG – Adventures at the Fairground
Project Manager: Lena Allblom, IKEA FAMILY
Project Co-ordinator: Anders Truedsson, IMP Books
Fact Checker: Fredrik Bengtsson, Children's IKEA Range Communicator
Text: Karin Salmson
Illustration: Andrea Dami/Tony Wolf
Typesetting: Gyllene Snittet
International editor: Janet Colletti, Boco Text Studio/Boco AB
Translation: Comactiva Translations AB, Sweden
Produced by IMP Books
Printing: Litopat, Italy
ISBN: 978-91-85727-41-4

It's today!

"Can… can… can…," stuttered the brown rabbit excitedly.

"I don't want to dance the can-can!" the small (though quite big) bulldog said grumpily. "I'm just about to shoot!"

The brown rabbit took a big breath and continued:
"Can you stop the game?"
The small bulldog did as the rabbit asked.
"Why?" she wondered.
"Yes, why?" repeated the white terrier.
"I just remembered what day it is today!" the brown rabbit replied.

Just then the cocker spaniel came running through the bushes, which hid the animals' football pitch from the humans.

"It's today!"

"Yes, we know it's *today*," sighed the little beige rabbit. "Can somebody please say something more than that it's *today* today? Because it's *today* every day, and I don't find that so special that I should stop playing football just when we're taking penalties. But if it was my birthday today, THEN…"

"Oh be quiet!" the cocker spaniel interrupted. "Today is the day the people on the farm take the day off…"

"Hooray!" cheered all the animals.

All apart from the guinea pig, who didn't always keep up. He looked confused.

"What?! Who won?"

"But sweetie…," the little golden retriever began.

"Do you think so? That's very kind…," said the guinea pig with a purr.

"No, yes… I mean, what I was about to say was that today is the day the people on the farm go to the fairground!"

The guinea pig got so excited, all he could say was:

"Oink, oink, oink." And: "Oink, oink, oink."

"You know what to do," hissed the big bulldog (and she really was big) to the other animals, who were all hiding behind the barn.

"When we're sure no one's watching the back of the truck, we have to be quick. The big ones help the little ones first. And once we're on we have to be absolutely silent!"

The animals nodded. They had done this before, because on one day every year, after the morning tasks, the people on the farm stopped what they were doing. They dressed up nicely and took the truck to the fairground in town.

Perhaps you find it strange that the animals are going

6

along? And perhaps it is strange. But that's the way it has been since the day a wise old lady took her two cats along to the fairground, because they had told her they love heights.

But now you're thinking cats can't tell people things, because cats can't talk. But that's where you're wrong! Animals can talk – it's just that us people can't listen. Most of us anyway. This wise old lady could listen to animals, so she let her cats come along to ride on the Ferris Wheel. Since then, generation after generation of animals on the farm have snuck along to the fairground.

The animals all huddled together under a big cover. The three mice kept looking at the cat siblings, feeling a bit worried.

"Don't worry," purred the grey cat in a friendly way. "Today we're all friends."

"Today we do nothing nasty to each other," the orange cat added with a purr.

"So who did this then?" the rat hissed angrily.

She gave a sniff in the air.

"Oh, sorry!" whimpered the poodle. He tried to move himself away from the others.

"I get so nervous and, well… then I seem to do rude noises!"

"Well this is certainly more than just a noise, it's terrible!" said the rat.

"Silence!" commanded the big golden retriever. "The people are coming!"

He was right. Soon the truck started up and the adventure could begin.

Little heroes

After a while on the back of the truck – nobody was sure how long as they had all fallen asleep – it came to a stop. The animals heard the people get out of the truck and then walk off chatting happily.

"The coast is clear!" said the grey cat as he peeped out from under the cover.

"We'll go to the hole in the fence together, then everyone can go off and do what they like."

"But don't forget, we all have to get straight back to the truck when the town hall clock strikes five," the big bulldog reminded them. "Can everyone count to five?"

"Count a fly? I can't even see a fly!" said the guinea pig, a bit confused. He hadn't really been listening.

"COUNT TO FIVE," said the beige rabbit slowly, adding with a sigh: "We meet back here when the clock strikes five!"

"Well everyone knows that! That's what we do every year!" snorted the guinea pig, offended.

Now you're probably wondering how a group of animals can just go running around a fairground. Well, as far back as anyone could remember, some animals had always turned up at the fair one day a year. In the beginning the people tried to chase them away, but after a few years it became a tradition, and the people thought it was nice to let the animals have some fun. No one really spoke about it, because they were afraid people in the town would think it was crazy. But they always kept the hole in the fence open.

And soon all the animals had gone through the hole, even the big bulldog.

"That hole's smaller than last year," she muttered.

"Either that or it's you that…" began the poodle, only to hear
an angry:

"Silence!"

"Muuuum," said the little bulldog. "Can we go off by
ourselves? Can we, please, pleeeaaase…"

"All right, as long as you remember to stay out of sight. And
you know the only person who doesn't let animals on their
ride is the lady with the Ghost Train, so keep away from there!"

"Yes yes, we know," shouted the little bulldog, the little
golden retriever and the cocker spaniel. But they were already
halfway to the popcorn stand.

11

Once they reached the popcorn stand, the three friends stopped. It was a great tradition to start a day at the fairground with popcorn. But there was a problem.

"Wonder who's on the stand today," said the cocker spaniel.

Because there were two brothers who ran the popcorn stand. One gave the animals as much popcorn as they could eat – almost. But the other one…

"Hmm, yes, the other one…" growled the little golden retriever. "He's so mean, he swallows his own burps!!"

The friends all burst into laughter.

"Hello there!" came a voice. "So you're here again are you?"

That was lucky. It was the nice brother who looked out at the giggling friends, and soon they were all sitting behind the stand feasting on popcorn.

Suddenly their peace and quiet was disturbed by a desperate *MIAOW*.

"Where did that come from?!" wondered the cocker spaniel.

She looked around worriedly.

"There!" puffed the little bulldog.

The grey cat was hanging from the Ferris Wheel. The orange cat was in one of the seats, hanging over the edge trying to reach him. But he was too far away.

"I can't… can't reach… it's too far!" howled the grey cat.

"Look!" yelled the little golden retriever. "The mice are running up!"

And they were. The quick little mice could go almost anywhere and they were now running up the Ferris Wheel's frame.

"But what can they do? They're too small," said the cocker spaniel worriedly.

But of course it's not always being biggest that matters – unless it's having the biggest heart. The mice had noticed there was a rope up there at the top. They quickly gnawed off a long piece, and working together they brought it over to the seat and the orange cat.

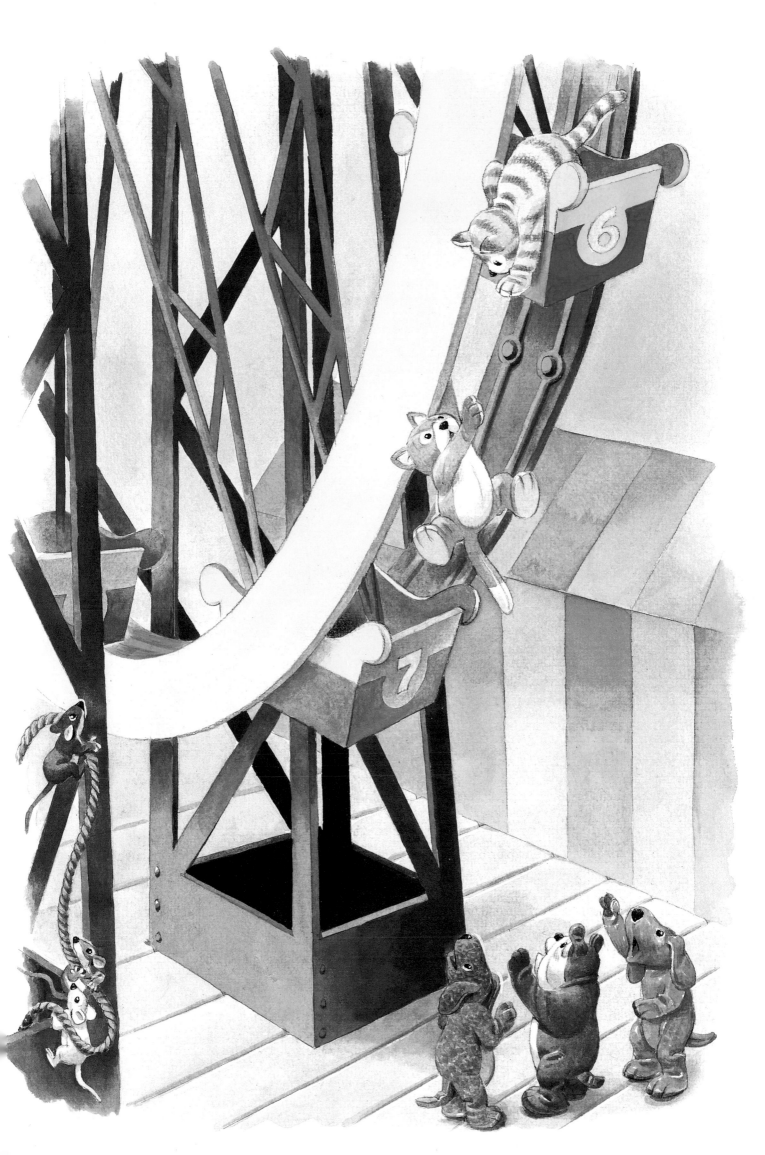

Together they lowered the rope down to the grey cat.

"But if I let go to grab the rope I'll fall," said the grey cat in despair.

"Hold this!" said the white mouse to the orange cat.

Then the three mice scampered down the rope.

"Hang in there," they said comfortingly and tied the rope around the grey cat's tummy.

16

"Pull up," they shouted to the orange cat.

When the Ferris Wheel had started moving again and the cats were safely back on the ground, all the friends were waiting.

"What happened?" wondered the poodle.

"Yes, what happened?" echoed the terrier.

"I was leaning a bit too far out," purred the grey cat, a little ashamed.

"If it hadn't been for the mice…"

"Do you know what," said the grey cat suddenly. "We shouldn't only be friends today. We promise never to chase you again."

She stroked the mice's heads with her soft tail.

"Ahh, that's nice!" said the terrier happily.

"But we're off to the Tunnel of Love. See you all later, alligator!"

Ghostly dogs

A little shaken, the cocker spaniel, the little bulldog and the little golden retriever walked behind the other dogs towards the Tunnel of Love.

"I don't want to go on the Tunnel of Love, do you?" asked the little bulldog.

"Nope… how about the Funhouse?" wondered the cocker spaniel.

The other dogs climbed into their boats while the three friends stayed put. Next door to the Tunnel of Love was the Ghost Train. The three looked at it longingly. But the angry lady was at the desk.

"She'll never let us ride the Ghost Train!" sighed the little golden retriever.

"No, not ride it maybe," said the cocker spaniel with a crafty smile.

"What do you mean?" wondered the others.

"Come on!" whispered the cocker spaniel, sneaking up to the opening where carriages full of screaming people came out every now and again.

"We may not be able to ride, but we can still take a look at the ghosts and other scary things!"

"Whoa, this is scary," giggled the little golden retriever as they vanished into the darkness.

It was pitch black inside.

"Go along the edge of the track and listen out for carriages. If one comes along we'll have to get out of the way," said the cocker spaniel.

"Woooooo!"

"Heeelp!" screamed the three friends in unison, before whooping with laughter.

A ghost had suddenly been lit up in the darkness.

"Come on, let's go on," laughed the cocker spaniel.

But then they heard the sound of a carriage.

"Oh! We need to get off the track," said the little golden retriever, adding:

"There's a space here!"

The three friends stood together and kept completely still and silent to make sure they were not seen.

The carriage drew closer, and just as it passed the dogs everything lit up again and a chilling laugh filled the air.

The ghost suddenly appeared behind the three friends again.

"Waaaaa!" screamed the people in the carriage which quickly passed by.

"Dad! That was… our dogs!" said a small voice as the carriage disappeared.

"It can't have been, they're at home," the man chuckled.

Once they were out of earshot the dogs breathed out – and then burst out laughing.

"We'd better get out of here so no one finds us."

In another part of the fairground the rabbits were having a great time in the Funhouse.

The guinea pig and the rat were having their tenth go on the Roller-Coaster,

and the cats were taking it easy on the Merry-Go-Round.

The mice were doing what they liked best – driving bumper cars. Except they weren't very good at it.

After a go on the Flume Ride, the dogs were thinking about what to do next.

"Am I the only one who fancies an ice-cream?" wondered the terrier.

He certainly wasn't the only one.

So the animals went off to the ice-cream café, which was run by a nice lady who loved animals. Especially dogs.

"I've been waiting for you!" she said delightedly when she saw the dogs.

"You'd like some ice-cream I suppose?"

The dogs wagged their tails happily and sat down nicely.

"I'd like chocolate sauce on mine," said the poodle.

"Okay!" answered the lady.

The animals looked at one another, confused. Did she just answer them?! Had she heard what the poodle said?

Anyway, she soon came back with vanilla and strawberry cones, with a big dollop of chocolate sauce for the poodle.

A skunk from the country

S oon – far too soon for the animals – the town hall clock sounded five dull chimes.

BONG. BONG. BONG. BONG. BONG.

"One, two, three, four, five," said the little bulldog, who liked counting.

"The people will be off to the truck now. We need to hurry so we get there before them," said the big bulldog, urging them on.

The poodle sighed.

"I shouldn't have eaten so much ice-cream and chocolate sauce. My tummy's bubbling and rumbling."

"Be careful!" said the rat who had joined the others on the way to the hole in the fence.

"Do what you did on the way here and you'll end up with your behind outside the cover."

"What's that?" wondered the guinea pig who had also turned up. "Who's ended up behind their brother?"

"No, I said…" the rat began. "Oh, never mind!"

As the animals approached the fence they realised something wasn't quite right. There were a lot of animals outside the fence. Dogs and cats, rats and even the occasional bird. They were looking in at the animals from the farm and did not look happy.

"What's going on?" whispered the beige rabbit. "Are they waiting for us?"

"I hope not!" said the big golden retriever with a worried voice.

But they were. When the animals reached the fence, one of the big dogs outside said:

"Aha! So you're the country folk we've heard so much about! Come here to enjoy yourselves have you?"

"Yes…" said the terrier, testing the ground. "Is that a problem…?"

"Yes!" growled one of the other dogs.

"Why?" asked the nosey guinea pig.

"BECAUSE!" hissed the cat outside the fence.

"Help!" yelped the little bulldog. "This is going to turn ugly."

"We need to get to the truck. Now!" said the big bulldog angrily. "We'll just have to try climbing through the fence. We can't let them stop us."

There seemed to be more and more animals on the outside as the farm animals climbed through the fence. Nervously, they stood still and looked at the town animals.

Suddenly there was a smell – actually a terrible stink. The worst stink you could ever imagine.

One of the town cats gave out a roar:

"They've got skunks with them!"

"Run!" howled the dogs.

The town animals were all over the place as they tried to get away, and soon the street was empty.

"Sorry about that…" said the poodle, clearing his throat. "I got scared and when I'm scared I… well I do even more rude noises!"

The other animals stared at the poodle.

"And there was all that ice-cream… and the chocolate sauce," the poodle continued.

"Wow!" said the cocker spaniel. "That was the worst one I've ever smelt. Impressive!"

"You saved us!" said the rat admiringly.

"Oh…," said the poodle, blushing.

"We'd better hurry to the truck!"

Shhh! They're asleep.

They certainly need it after a day like that. Yes, they made it before the humans, because the humans were a bit slower than normal. They were chatting about whether there could possibly be dogs in the Ghost Train. And if so, could it possibly be their dogs? But of course they realised that's absolutely impossible.

But we know better, don't we?

Even so, maybe it's a good thing that this day only comes once a year. There's enough adventure back on the farm for all the other days, but you'll hear about that another time.